Offering

Robin Deffendall

The bell hanging from the door handle jangled in a decidedly unmusical tone as Chief of Police Mark Brandon opened the door to Junior's Auto Repair. He'd stopped by after happening upon Junior's wife Ruby on the street in front of the Piggly Wiggly. Her obvious unease was evident in their brief chat, so before taking his leave he shook her hand, seeking delicately for some reason for this. That touch left Brandon with an instant and powerful feeling that he should stop by the shop about five o'clock.

"Hey, Junior," he called into the bay. The man looked up and wiped the grease from his hands on a dirty rag. He stood, stretched and joined Brandon in the office. The Sheriff frowned slightly as he shook Junior's hand. He looked back over his shoulder, scanning the street and the tiny parking lot in front of the shop.

"What can I do for you, Chief?"

"Well, it's been a while since I've been by. I just thought I'd drop in, do a little community policing. Things have been pretty slow in the mayhem department lately."

"Well, it can't be all fun and games, can it?"

"Nope. In fact, I prefer it calm," Brandon said. Most of the Chief's job involved ensuring the bars emptied out in the general vicinity of two a.m. and that the drivers were able to make it home without incident. He knew—had always known—that he was uniquely qualified to prevent crime. With his special skill set, enforcement was rarely needed. In fact, he had never been required to use, much less draw his gun in the line of duty. Instead he made it his duty to keep tabs on the troublemakers. When he got wind of something about to ignite, he made damn sure he was there to quietly put a stop to it before someone needed to go to jail. As a result, other than testosterone-fueled fist fights and a neighborly feud now and then, the majority of the department's calls arose from barking dogs, loud parties and the occasional carload of rowdy teens playing mailbox baseball. Younger deputies would have been bored, but the Chief had deliberately hired John Elmer and Duke Fisher because they were seeking the quiet of a small town to raise their young families. The Chief worked very hard to ensure Virden stayed that dull. It was this self-appointed responsibility that brought Brandon to Junior's Auto Repair at 4:54 p.m.

He propped up the counter with his left hip and began the traditional small town news exchange. The two men discussed all the important matters—weather, last night's football game, whether someone needed to lose their job over the dam that had collapsed and been replaced and collapsed again. When the niceties had been sufficiently covered, Brandon checked his watch. Just about time.

A decrepit Jeep colored mostly gray from poorly sprayed primer lurched to a stop in the parking lot and Billy Curtis emerged. Brandon looked him over as he entered the office. He was hunched into a dark grey hooded sweat jacket, his hands deep in the pockets. Dressed far too warmly for the hot August evening. His eyes were watery and bloodshot, matching the red of his face. The man looked sick. Or intensely nervous.

Junior raised his hands toward Billy and moved to block his entry. "Billy, we talked about this. You can't be here anymore."

"You owe me, man."

"No, Billy." Junior gestured toward Brandon. "I told you if you left I wouldn't drag the law into it. You don't want to bring this up in front of the Chief, now, do you?"

Curtis' eyes darted his direction seeming to see him for the first time. Chief Brandon rose to his most imposing height. He strolled over, his tension disguised beneath a casual outward demeanor. "How are you doing, Billy?" He stuck his hand out and, perhaps out of habit, the man shook it. Brandon reached through the handshake and *pulled*, and felt a tremor move across the clammy grip.

"Ok, I guess," Billy mumbled, not making eye contact. He shuffled his feet.

"Got a minute?" Brandon used the hand shake to subtly turn Billy towards the door, and added a friendly arm across his shoulders to further urge him towards the exit. "I wanted to talk to you about something before you get away."

Curtis allowed himself to be steered out the door and back into the parking lot. Brandon placed himself between the man and Junior's shop door. "I heard about your problem." The Chief spoke quietly. His hand resting on Billy's arm helped to focus the man's inebriated attention. "You know you can't blame Junior. You stole money from him. He had to fire you."

He looked up at Brandon, his eyes uncomprehending. "Who…? How do you…?"

"Don't worry about how. What's important is I know," Brandon said. "The same as I know that .22 in your pocket isn't going to help anything."

Billy's eyes widened and his hand went to his pocket almost without thought.

"Yes, I know about that, too. How you're planning to make Junior feel a little of the pain you've been feeling. Get a little retribution. But it won't do any good. It's just gonna make you feel bad about it when the beers wear off. He's your brother-in-law, Billy. You can't stick a gun in his face. What would Ruby say?"

Billy's blush betrayed his embarrassment. "I wasn't—"

"Why don't you give it to me?" Brandon said gently. He held his hand out between the two of them, low so no one would see what passed between them.

"Come on, Billy. Besides, you didn't even load it. It won't do you a helluva lot of good when Junior pulls out that cannon he keeps behind the counter. You would just make him shoot you and then he'd feel like shit and I'd have to check you out of the hospital just to throw your drunk ass in jail."

One tear escaped and ran down Billy Curtis' face. "I ruin everything. I can't even do this right."

"No, Billy," Brandon said. "This *is* right. Give me the gun. You don't need something like that. Makes you think bad thoughts."

Curtis slipped the .22 out of his pocket and pressed the handle into the Chief's hand. "We'll just keep this between the two of us, OK? No one else needs to know." Brandon dropped the gun quietly into his pocket. "I'll give it back to you in a couple of days," he said.

Curtis wiped a finger under his nose.

Brandon slapped him on the back. "Good man," he said. "Tomorrow, when you've had some time to think about things a bit, I want you to come into the office and we'll talk over some options. I may have a couple of suggestions for places you can apply for work."

"Thanks, Chief." Curtis gave him a weak smile.

"You're not a bad man, Billy. You just needed a bit of a reminder is all. Now, go on home and give Ruby a kiss. She's waiting dinner for you."

Curtis turned, lifting his elbows to balance carefully.

"And Billy—?" the man paused and looked up at the Chief. "Let me have the car keys, too. I'll give you a ride home."

Later that night Chief Brandon climbed out of his patrol car in front of a bar on the edge of Virden's business district. Dick's was a local dive that, rumor said, was named more for its rough clientele than the owner. When the economy tanked and the drinkers grew surlier, the bar had become part of the Chief's regular handshake patrols. It was a good venue for intelligence gathering in Brandon's one-man War on Crime.

He took a moment for his eyes to adjust to the dim interior before moving through the after-work crowd, the miners and the mechanics, the bikers and the bar bums. He greeted each by name with a handshake or a touch on the shoulder. "How are you, Jimmy? Malik? Everything good for you, Caleb?"

He stopped next to Martin, put a heavy hand on his shoulder and felt his nerves tingle at his pull. "When are you going to replace that left front tire, Martin? We talked about this last week. No sense in having an accident. It would be a shame to lose control on the way to work and plow into a telephone pole. Promise you'll get it changed right away."

"Chief, I ain't got money for that 'til next payday. Or after. It'll be OK until then."

"No, it won't. Get a retread if you have to, but get it done tomorrow."

"Chief—"

"Tomorrow morning, Martin. Or I'll write you up for a safety violation. How much you in for here?" Brandon asked. He counted the glasses and did a quick mental calculation then flipped a twenty onto the table. "I'll pick up your tab tonight and that'll help you towards that retread. Do it, Martin."

"OK. OK."

Brandon shook his head. Martin had no intention of replacing that tire any time soon. His twenty would probably pay for another round for the table. He shook a few more hands, completing his circuit and headed towards the bar.

Ginger leaned over the worn counter and gave Brandon a quick, serviceable kiss. "Hey, G," he greeted her with an easy familiarity. They had been dating for six or seven years, and living together for maybe three of those, and they were talking about the next step. Should they get married? Did she even want to commit to a man who would always give more of himself to his community than he would to her? It was a big decision. Brandon could easily have pulled the answer from her through some casual contact, but he refused to violate her trust. He would wait for her to tell him herself.

"What'll it be tonight, Chief?" Ginger was already

filling a glass with ice. She always asked, though she always knew the answer to the question.

"Jack and Coke."

She handed him the soda and neither commented on its virginity. They both knew the routine. He smiled at her and she replied with a smile that never failed to quicken his heartbeat. "See you at two?" she asked.

"Affirmative," he replied. She kissed him again before he turned back to his business.

Brandon paused in front of a tired-looking woman in scrubs decorated with frolicking kittens. Lindsay Callahan was a single mom who had moved back home to live with her mother after her husband had cleaned out their joint bank account and filed for divorce. Brandon felt her frustration as he took her hand. He asked her about her day.

She waggled her glass of beer. "I could tell you stories, but you don't want to know. Trust me."

"How's your mother, Lindsay?" He looked in her eyes. "I understand she's not doing well."

Lindsay blinked. "She's been feeling poorly lately. She says she gets tired a lot. I came home from my 14-hour shift yesterday and she was taking a nap while little Bennie was wandering all around the house. At eleven o'clock at night! He's seven years old for crying out loud. He can't be left to fend for himself. He gets into everything. I wish I could hire a decent babysitter."

"Nobody got hurt, though." It was a statement, not a question.

"No, he wasn't hurt, but he tried to make his own dinner. You should have seen my kitchen. The microwave looked like a cat had exploded in it. If she can't take care of my kid any better than that, I may have to kill her."

"Careful, now." He tapped the badge on his chest. "Anything you say…"

She laughed as the tension drained from her shoulders.

"Is she always like that? I mean, you're a nurse. You must've seen this sort of thing. What if it's something bad, like her heart? You want to get her looked at real soon. Find out what's wrong. Promise me you will."

"You're right, Chief. I shouldn't have flipped out. I was just so tired. I'll head home as soon as I finish my beer and check her out."

"Good girl." He patted her hand and moved on.

Brandon was driving west on Porter Avenue the next afternoon when he saw the AT&T truck parked next to a canted telephone pole. Skid marks in the shoulder told the story. "Dammit, Martin," he muttered and turned his cruiser around to head back toward the hospital.

He found Martin in Emergency Bay 2 where Lindsay was wrapping his arm with plastered gauze.

He removed his shades and pierced Martin with a steely gaze. "Too busy to stop by the tire shop this morning, Martin?"

Martin hung his head. "I know. You don't have to say it."

"Well, apparently I do have to say it."

"I'm sorry."

"Yes. You are. Now your car is totaled and your arm is busted. You'll be out of work for what?"

"Six weeks. At least." Lindsay supplied.

"All because it was more important to sleep off last

night's drunk than to buy a new tire."

Martin winced as Lindsay adjusted his arm into a sling.

"Did Duke write you up for the safety violation like I told him?"

"Yes."

"Alright then. Next time I tell you something, Martin, you can believe what I say."

"Yes, sir."

Lindsay followed him out of the bay, drawing the curtain behind her. "Chief," she called after him. "I heard you tell Martin to fix that tire. It did blow out this morning, just like you said it would. How'd you know about that?"

"I'm a police officer, Lindsay. We're paid to notice things like that."

"And my mother. You knew she was sick."

He just looked at her, not sure how to respond.

"When she finally told me she was having intermittent chest pains I called the ambulance and the next thing I know they're giving her nitroglycerin. She has angina."

"Really?"

Her eye brows were pinched together and her fingers twitched at her name badge. "So how did you know? You said she might be having heart trouble."

"Did I? I guess it was a lucky guess." Brandon touched her shoulder and gave a tiny mental *pull*. "But I'm sure she's going to be OK, Lindsay," he said. He wanted to tell her not to worry so much, but after that brief touch Brandon knew that she had some worry coming. And her mother's heart was the least of it.

Chief Brandon drove directly to Franklin Elementary School to verify the impression Lindsay had given him outside the emergency room.

He stood staring at the playground where Mrs. Montgomery's class was enjoying 45 minutes of undirected activity. Children swarmed over monkey bars and merry-go-rounds. A group of four boys were playing a game of two-on-two basketball that didn't seem to have any discernible rules. Others sat laughing on benches in twos and threes. In a corner of the playground he found the one he'd been looking for. From the reading he'd had when he touched her, he recognized Lindsay's son, Bennie, stooping under a pine tree. He seemed to be looking for something in the pine straw. There. He'd found it and slipped the thing into the pocket of his shorts.

He returned to the larger group, stopping briefly to speak to the basketball players. One of the boys tucked the ball under a cocked arm and they all turned to watch Bennie as he targeted two girls sitting nearby. Jessica Mills and Tiffany Edwards were nearly indistinguishable, sitting with their heads together and their frilly pink dresses spread carefully across the bench. They even swung their identical black patent leather Mary Janes in unison. Destined to be cheerleaders and prom queens, Brandon was sure of it.

Bennie spoke briefly to the girls who looked up expectantly.

Then he reached into the pocket and removed the thing he'd found. A green garden snake, slim and writhing. Jessica pulled back in alarm, but Tiffany leaped up and fled screaming. Bennie chased her, holding the snake toward her at arm's-length as she shrieked in terror. In the moment before Mrs. Montgomery could intervene, Bennie had the girl trapped in a corner where the walls of two classrooms met. Tiffany shrank into a fetal ball, tears streaming down her face. "No, Bennie! *No!*"

Bennie threw the snake at her and Tiffany began kicking her feet and beating her hands against her face, her hair, her chest. Mrs. Montgomery was there an instant too late, followed closely by the Chief who had needed to race around the fence to the gate before he could gain access. The teacher enfolded the child in her arms, making soothing noises and restraining her against further hysterics.

Brandon was panting as he stopped near the two. "Can I help?" he asked.

Mrs. Montgomery looked up at him. Her face was stone still and there was a line of white around her lips. She said, "Will you speak with Bennie? I don't think I can do it right now." She jerked her head meaningfully toward a stain spreading over Tiffany's pristine skirt. "Besides, I need to clean her up a little and get her to the office so her mom can take her home."

"Sure, no problem," Brandon said.

"Thanks, Chief." She spoke briefly to her aide then rose, took the girl's hand and the two made a regal and dignified exit from the field.

Bennie was laughing with the boy with the basketball. Brandon crooked a finger at him, summoning him into the presence of The Law. The boy dutifully walked over, his eyes wide and innocent. He was like any other seven-year-old. Jeans cut off just above the knees, tee shirt bearing the logo of the superhero *du jour*. Bright blond hair buzzed close. Brandon towered over him in the way only the Chief of Police can.

"What was that all about?" he asked.

"Huh?"

"That thing with the snake. What was up with the snake?"

"I was showing it to her."

"You were chasing her with it."

The boy looked down at his feet, but Brandon had seen the sparkle in his eyes.

"She was screaming, Bennie. She said, 'No.' She said, 'Stop.' Why didn't you stop?"

Bennie shrugged. Kids never knew why they did anything.

"Come over here, Bennie." Brandon indicated a nearby bench and they both sat. "I'm gonna explain some things to you. This is important, and you need to remember it for the rest of your life, OK?"

The boy nodded.

"Girls don't like snakes, Bennie." He shook his head. "They don't like them one bit. They're scared of snakes,"

Brandon looked hard for any sign of empathy or regret from the boy and found none. He tried again. "Are you afraid of anything, Bennie?"

The boy thought for a moment. He didn't seem to come up with anything.

"How about a tiger?" Brandon asked him. "If a tiger came onto the playground, would you be afraid?"

"Uh-uh." There was no hesitation.

"No? A tiger?"

"Nope. I'd just run really fast. Over there where they're playing dodge ball. Cause I can run a lot faster than Jimmy Phelps."

The boy seemed to be serious. He hadn't even paused to think about it. Brandon sighed.

"You see, Bennie, the things we do show what kind of a person we are. You can choose to be a good person, or you can choose to be a bad person, understand? You do good things and people think you're a good man. You do bad things and how do you think people think about you?"

"That you're a bad man?"

"Right." Now he was making progress. "And when you were chasing Tiffany, did you think that was a good thing? Did you think that was funny?"

The boy's eyes lit up. "Yeah, did you see her?"

"I didn't think it was funny. I thought it was mean." Instantly the boy's face became guarded and he looked away.

"Do you want to be a bad person, Bennie?"

"No."

"The thing is, when a girl—when any person, but *especially* a girl—when they say no, it means no. *Always.* Understand?"

Bennie nodded.

"OK, then. I need you to promise me, Bennie. Promise you'll remember this forever." He didn't want to do it. Not to a kid. He felt like it was a violation, but he had to know. He stuck out his hand to shake. "Promise me."

As the boy took his hand Brandon *pulled* and felt the charge he always felt travel up his arm. He let go immediately and took a half-step back. The current was wrong. The strange current that carried with it all the person's secrets, past and future had not flowed liquid and smooth from Bennie to Brandon like it did with most everyone else. His fizzled and crackled, skipping brokenly from neuron to neuron. He got none of the unusual indicators of some developing mean streak from the boy. He'd felt that often enough since beginning his handshake patrols, so he knew what to look for. But there was no sense of what Brandon thought of as Humanity, either. The boy was… hollow. Isolated glimpses of branching futures fluttering through his mind. But none seemed to coalesce into any significant incident. So many possibilities leading in myriad directions, but he knew they would all end the same. Brandon had felt this once before. But only once.

"Are you OK, Mister?

Chief Mark Brandon stood and walked briskly away. The classroom aide made eye contact and opened her mouth to speak, then closed it again. Brandon continued around the corner of the building, found the nearest trash can and retched.

Ginger found him later that night at the kitchen table sitting with his head propped on the palms of his hands. Embarrassed, he nearly tried to hide the tumbler of Jack Daniels that sat near his elbow. But he knew her practiced eye would measure the level of bourbon missing from the fresh bottle and find it matched the amount in the glass. She would know he hadn't drunk any of it.

Ginger ran her hand across his shoulders as she crossed behind him to pull out a chair. They sat in silence for a moment. When he didn't speak she said carefully, "When I didn't see you before closing, I was worried."

He stirred then, wiped his drawn face with one hand. "Sorry. You can get rid of this." He handed her the tumbler. She picked up the bottle too, and poured both into the sink.

"Rough day?" she asked

He grunted. "Understatement."

"Want to talk?"

"Not really."

She sat down at the table again, patient.

Finally, "About eight years ago I arrested a man. Chester Bonaventure. I still remember his name. He was just as normal-seeming as anybody. Had a good job downtown. Went to church. Took care of his momma. Nobody had any clue that he had raped and killed five prostitutes and dumped them in the creek outside of town. The things he'd done to them, Ginger... And nobody even suspected him."

He looked up but he wasn't seeing her anymore.

"Duke's the one that caught him, so I didn't have any opportunity to read him at first. But I had to. I couldn't take the risk that he might not be the guy. So I made sure I was the one who took the cuffs off before we put him in the cell. God, I wish I hadn't touched him.

"I can't explain it. I saw everything he had done to those girls. Every goddamn perverted thing. But that isn't what gives me nightmares." He shook his head. "Ginger, that man wasn't normal at all. Not on any level. He was... *wrong*. There was some big piece—some important piece—that was missing. Some piece that made him like the rest of us. Without it he didn't have

15

any off button. He could do the most horrific things and then stop by a café on the way home and order a slice of apple pie like nothing had happened. Doctors called him a sociopath. Like giving it some medical name made it better some how."

Brandon stopped again for a long time while Ginger sat silently holding his hand. Finally he inhaled, letting it out with a whoosh.

"I read a kid today. A seven year old boy. Tow headed. Just as cute as anything. And I know how his life is going to be. I can't tell you how the whole thing will play out, but I can tell you it won't be good. 'Cause the feeling I got when I touched him was the same.

"It was exactly the same."

There was a long silence. "So what are you going to do about it?" Her voice was quiet.

"What *can* I do? Tell his mother? 'Lady, I have seen the future and your kid is destined to become Jeffrey Dahmer?' Would you believe that if it was your kid?" He made a derisive noise. "More likely I'll be eating breakfast and there will come a knock at my door. It'll be the guys in white coats come to fit me for one of those jackets with the wrap-around sleeves."

"You can't just *not* tell her. She needs to know her son needs extra guidance, extra monitoring."

"I know" he said wearily. "I'll talk to her when she gets off work tomorrow. But I don't know what good it will do."

Brandon found Lindsay Callahan taking her lunchbreak at the pizza joint down the street from the hospital. He crossed directly to her table, forgoing his usual handshaked greetings with the other diners. She looked up at him over a slice of pepperoni.

"Hi, Lindsay. Mind if I sit down?"

"Sure," she said warily.

He slid into the seat across the booth from her. "I wanted to take a minute to talk to you about Bennie."

"What about Bennie?" She sat up straight and her voice lifted in alarm.

"The incident yesterday—"

She lifted her hand to stop him. "I heard all about it this morning. I had to take two hours off work—two hours I could not afford—to listen to *that principal* call my son a bully. A bully. My son!"

"Well, he did seem a little too gleeful after he threw the snake at the little girl."

"He's a boy. Boys do that kind of thing."

"Yes, but—"

"My son is not a bully. He's a kind, generous little boy." She said this with all the strength and force of unwavering maternal love. Brandon knew he would never convince her otherwise. "This morning he brought me an ant he found in the garden. He watched it walk up and down his arm for an hour until I made him take it outside. That's not a bully."

He moved on to Plan B. "I'm not saying Bennie is a bad kid." *I'm not saying it, just thinking it.* "I'm just saying that he might benefit from a strong male influence."

"And you're applying for the job?"

"I'm offering is all, if you think it would help."

"He has a father. He's a loser and jerk, but he's still Bennie's father."

"I don't want to be his father."

"And I just got free of one husband. I don't need a boyfriend right now."

17

"Lindsay, you are a beautiful woman and a lovely person, but I have a girlfriend. This is about Bennie. He's a good kid…"—*yeah, right*—"…and he may be acting out because he doesn't have your ex around. I'm not talking about moving into your life. I'm thinking, take him for an ice cream cone now and then. Maybe to the ballpark for a game."

Her eyes narrowed. "Why on earth would you want to spend time with someone else's kid?"

He could tell she was thinking unwholesome thoughts. "It's called 'community policing,' Lindsay, and it's why I became a police officer."

He could see her face and shoulders beginning to relax. He threw in the clincher. "Besides, I could check on your mother every so often, too. I know you must be worrying about her."

Her eyes began to tear up and he put a comforting hand on her arm and read her response. He was in.

Brandon started taking his lunch break at 3:30. He parked under a shade tree in front of the Callahan's rental to eat a couple of peanut butter and jellies washed down with the remaining coffee in his morning thermos. Maybe if he added Bennie to his daily handshake patrol, everything would be OK.

It had always worked for him in the past. Virden was a safe, even a boring, town precisely because he'd always been able to persuade most of the local petty criminals away from their intended malfeasance. One reading and he knew where it would go down and how. Sure it took some fast talking and all of his persuasive powers sometimes, but for the most part he was successful. He knew most people weren't truly bad.

They just made bad decisions, so he made it his duty to help them in that area. It didn't always work. Sometimes the alcohol or pharmaceuticals won out over reason. In those cases he could easily arrest them after the fact. And all it took was a touch.

So if he could just casually touch Bennie every day or so, he hoped he could safeguard the town from this seven year old... monster-in-waiting.

Bennie's bus halted at the corner and the boy emerged with two other children, ten year old Jenny and a boy Bennie's age. One of the many Greenfield kids. The boys spoke animatedly for a moment and then each turned toward their respective homes.

Brandon stepped out onto the sidewalk. "Hi, Bennie. Remember me? My name is Chief Brandon." *That was probably the wrong tactic,* he thought. "You can call me Mark, though. Your mom asked me to make sure you got home from school safely."

"My mom didn't say that."

Damn. Kid's sharp. "No, you're right. I think she really wanted me to check on your grandmother. She's a little worried about her."

Bennie narrowed his eyes.

"She said you could trust police officers, didn't she?"

"Yeah."

"Well..." he gestured towards his badge. Bennie shrugged and headed home.

"How was school today?"

"OK."

"You see the WWE championship bout last weekend?

"My mom doesn't let me watch that. She says it's too violent. I think it's really because it's too expensive."

"I see." That about covered the conversation during the walk to the front door.

Bennie unlocked the door with a key he pulled from his backpack.

"Grandma! I'm home!" He dumped his backpack at the foot of the stairs and headed for the kitchen.

"Can I come in?" Brandon called after him.

The boy shrugged and Brandon took that as an invitation.

As did many law enforcement officers, Brandon had the habit of surveying any new environs. He roamed from room to room, looking. He wasn't sure what he expected to see. Finger paintings of axe murders? A couple of pipe bombs on the bathroom sink? There was nothing to alarm him. It was just a slightly cluttered, normal house.

In the back bedroom he found the grandmother. She was sitting on the edge of her bed watching a courtroom reality show. A grey Persian sat on her lap, receiving her attentions as if entitled.

Brandon knocked on her open door. "Mrs. Callahan?"

The old woman jumped, and the cat did too, rubbing itself dramatically against the door jamb before strutting out the room.

He introduced himself, shaking her hand to satisfy his duty to check up on her health. She was doing quite well after her surgery.

"You must be the cop Lindsay said was going to stop by."

"Yes, Ma'am."

"Don't 'Ma'am' me. My name is Olivia. Liv. Are you going to be checking up on Lindsay, too?"

"No, Ma'am. I figure she can take care of herself."

"Well, she can't."

"No?"

"That girl needs a man in the worst way. You should take her out."

"I'm flattered you think I'm good enough for her. She's a remarkable woman."

"Yes, she is. So don't wait too long, hear?" The commercial was over and she turned back to her television.

He found Bennie in the kitchen hastily brushing Fig Newton crumbs off his shirt. Brandon made no reference to the subterfuge, but the silent message that passed between them said that he knew and would keep the secret.

He put out his hand to shake.

Nothing. Brandon's reading gave him no disturbing images, but he also did not sense that indescribable something. The boy remained empty. Void.

In nearly every way the boy was completely average, with ambitions and concerns typical of any seven year old kid. There was a perfect place to build a club house in the woods down by the creek, if only he could score some lumber. Amy Brewer was having a party on Saturday and Bennie planned to give her his Barrel of Monkeys as a gift. He didn't use them anymore anyway. Jimmy Phelps had farted during dodge ball today and everyone laughed.

Yep. Typical. Today Bennie was up to nothing more malevolent than sneaking a Fig Newton while his grandmother was distracted by Judge Alex.

He breathed a sigh of relief. "Thank you, Bennie," he said. "I appreciate you letting me drop in. Say 'hi' to your mother for me."

The boy nodded, unable to speak around his mouthful of cookies.

And so the handshake patrols continued.

After school Brandon would visit with Bennie for about fifteen minutes, ensuring that he shook the boy's hand before leaving. Bennie seemed to enjoy the camaraderie, and the ego boost these brief touches gave him. No one else asked him to shake hands like a man. A bond was forged.

Every day the Chief went home relieved that nothing unexpected was underway. Every day for almost a year. Eventually he allowed himself to be talked into taking a vacation.

Ginger had asked him to accompany her to a friend's wedding in Cincinnati. She had pleaded and he had finally relented. He owed her. He had neglected her too many nights in favor of what she had termed his new obsession. They had planned two days for the wedding and visiting, and a few extra days to vacation. Five days in all.

She said Brandon had needed some time away from the stress of constant vigilance and worry over Bennie. He had agreed, but he found he couldn't relax. He tried to think about Ginger, to focus on her and to live in the moment. To let himself have some fun. For her part she had tried her best to keep a constant stream of visitors and activities to keep his mind engaged. It did no good.

He managed to make it through the wedding but his unease continued to build steadily. He had not checked in on Bennie in several days.

Brandon walked from the window, around the blandly decorated room, to the door. He looked out the peephole briefly then sat on the edge of the nondescript comforter that covered the sterile white hotel sheets. He stood and picked up the television remote and started flipping channels. He couldn't focus.

At the reception, in the middle of a conversation about the bride's family, there had been a mention of children and Brandon's mind flew back to Bennie again. What was he doing? Was he getting into trouble? What if something should happen while Brandon was away?

While watching the white tiger and her cubs at the Cincinnati Zoo his mind had gone to the striped kitten Bennie had brought home and what the kitten had been intended for. Brandon spoke to Lindsay about it, but it wasn't until Liv's cat displayed some aggression toward the energetic ball of fluff that Bennie's mother had agreed. Brandon gave the kitten to Ginger. She didn't have to ask why.

His tension had built over the previous three days until now he couldn't sit still. He prowled around the room, muttering. He looked up and saw Ginger. She sat stiffly in a chair by the window, drumming her fingers on the round table.

"I'm sorry," Brandon said. "I really am trying."

Her reply was flinty. "Try harder."

"Ginger, you know I can't. You know why."

"He's not your son, Mark." He opened his mouth and she stopped him. "No. He is not your responsibility, either."

"What would you have me do, Ginger? Let him run amok?"

She threw up her hands. "He's not running amok,

Mark! He's being a little boy. Kids do mean things sometimes. It's part of growing up. Besides nothing has happened in a whole year. Nothing!"

"Because I've been there. Because I'm watching."

"Maybe. Maybe nothing will happen anyway. No matter what you do. Did you ever think of that?"

He looked up at her, startled by the revelation. She didn't believe. She didn't trust in his ability. She didn't trust him. He plopped down in the chair across the table from her.

She registered his hurt. He could see that. Her tone softened. "What if—even if—something were to happen and you couldn't stop it from happening? How would that make you feel? It would kill you. You know it. Maybe— maybe you shouldn't go out looking for trouble. Maybe you aren't meant to find out before—"

"Maybe not, but I do know. I can't unknow it. And I can't live with myself if I don't try to stop it."

"You work fourteen-hour days and then you spend all day with the kid every weekend. Seven days a week! I never see you. You look like walking death. When was the last time you had a full night's sleep?"

"I know. I know, but—"

"No buts. Look what that boy is doing to you. Look what it's doing to us. Mark, you need to give yourself a break."

"OK, OK."

She took his hand in hers. Quietly she said, "You can't be everyone's savior, Mark."

He looked out the window at the passing traffic. They didn't talk again that night.

They went home the next day, two days before the

scheduled end of their trip.

The following day Brandon redistributed his staff to arrange for an open School Resource Officer position at Franklin Elementary School. Then he resigned his position, turning in his Chief's badge for a uniform and a beat guarding Bennie and his school during the day. It left him with a regular schedule, more nights off and a twenty thousand dollar a year drop in pay. Ginger was right. He needed to give himself a break, and now he could do that and still see Bennie every day. He could be on the playground when he was out with his class. He could make that subtle touch that he needed like a fix—that he needed to be able to go home at night and breathe freely.

But summers meant he had to find excuses to stop by the boy's house.

On one sunny summer afternoon, Brandon found Bennie hunched over something in the dark corner of the flower bed where the perpetual shade of a pine tree left the area cool and damp.

Brandon walked quietly up behind him. The boy held a silver-topped salt shaker in his left hand. He flipped over a stone and liberally shook the shaker over it.

Brandon leaned over him to see what was so engrossing. In the middle of the exposed damp stone, a small mound of bubbles erupted.

"What's going on, Bennie?"

Bennie started and stood. "Huh?"

"What are you doing?"

"Playing. Grandma said go play in the yard. She's watching her court shows."

Brandon gestured at the salt shaker. "What are you

doing with that?"

"Salting slugs."

"What do you mean 'salting slugs'?"

"I saw it on YouTube. Want to see? Look."

He turned over another rock and shook the shaker over a huge slug that clung to the underside. The slug began to boil with a mucousy foam, squirming in distress.

"See? It's cool." Bennie looked up. His smile faded when he saw Brandon' face. "What?"

"What did that slug ever do to you?"

Bennie looked down at the foaming creature that was now struggling to escape the salt encrusting its body. "It's just a slug."

"It's just a living thing and you're torturing it." Brandon poured the remainder of his bottled water over the slugs, washing most of the salt crystals away.

"Mom doesn't like slugs in her garden. She said so."

"Then your mom can kill them. Cleanly. You don't torture them and watch them die slowly. Nothing should die like that. Even slugs."

The boy frowned and stood up again. Brandon put his hand out and Bennie dutifully placed the salt shaker in his hand. "Let's go inside and see your grandmother," he said. He put his hand on the back of Bennie's head, urging him toward the house.

The touch left no question. Bennie had no understanding that causing suffering was wrong in any way. And he certainly felt no remorse.

"Can I have some ice cream today?" Bennie asked.

"No, you cannot."

It was less than a week later when Brandon saw

Bennie again. With school out for the summer he had a regular beat and a cruiser. He had taken to driving past the Callahan house several times a day as he made his rounds. Duke, now in the awkward position of supervising his former boss, was starting to make comments and even Brandon was coming to realize his interest in the child was becoming unhealthy at best. But he had to keep track of the boy. The slug torture incident was just another example of how the boy seemed to be obsessed with learning how to wield vicious power over others. Sure it had just been slugs, but the glee in the child's eyes...

He rounded the corner onto Bennie's street and found the boy leaning against a picket fence surrounding a well-manicured lawn and a clapboard house with peeling blue paint. As he watched, Bennie picked up a stone from the edging of the flower bed and chucked it in a looping arc at a black Great Dane that stood silently at the far side of the lawn. The rock hit the dog in the shoulder and it yipped, leaping sideways several feet. It ran in a tight circle, looking for an escape route, but there was none. It had put itself in a corner. It stopped in a quivering crouch.

Bennie picked up another stone and cocked his arm again.

Brandon threw his cruiser into park and leaped from his seat. "What are you doing?" His voice cracked with authority.

Bennie lowered his arm but said nothing.

"Young man, I am so disappointed with you." He was using his Voice of Authority again. It worked with most kids.

Bennie just stood, his face impassive, looking off to

the left toward where the dog still cowered.

"Let's go." Bennie looked back at him. Brandon could see the calculations happening behind his eyes. No doubt he was trying to work out how much trouble he was in. Perhaps working out an explanation. Brandon grabbed him by the back of the neck and perp-walked him up the sidewalk to the front door of the house.

A woman dressed in sweat pants and a pink tank top, answered his knock. She was carrying an open historical novel. Brandon introduced himself and Bennie. "Well, Bennie," he prompted.

The boy tried what seemed to work for him most often. "I'm sorry."

The woman looked up confused. "Sorry for what, honey?"

Brandon gave him no help. Eventually the boy confessed. "I threw rocks at your dog."

Her hand flew to her chest and her voice raised an octave or two. "Prince? You threw rocks at Prince? Is he OK?" She stepped onto the porch trying to peer around the corner into the back yard.

"I think he's OK for the most part," Brandon told her. "I think he'll be fine."

She exhaled a ragged breath then turned around again. "How dare you throw rocks at my dog, you little brat. Why would you do that?"

Bennie shrugged. "He was barking at me. I was afraid. I wanted him to stay away."

Her face turned from the white of shock to a cloudy red. "I didn't hear any barking. And Prince is not a mean dog. You were just throwing rocks at a sweet dog to be mean. That's all.

"I better not see you in my yard *ever*. Do you understand? I don't want you anywhere on my property. If you ever come back here again, I'll call the cops and have them throw your juvenile ass in jail, do you hear me? And if I find out you hurt him, I am going to sue your mother for every dime she has. How *dare* you!" She paused for breath then got very still. "Get off my porch."

"Go sit in the car, Bennie," Brandon said. He turned back to the woman and spoke quietly and reasonably. "I'm sorry, ma'am. I'm sure he's fine, but if you do see anything that requires a vet, please let me know. I hope he's not too traumatized. You might want to check on him. I'll speak to Bennie's mother. Let her know. I wanted you to know what happened."

Her response was frigid. "Thank you, Officer Brandon." She shut the door to go check on her dog.

Brandon felt weighed down as he walked back to the car. Despite all his efforts, Bennie was failing. He did not seem to have any empathy. None at all. He seemed to enjoy playing the vengeful god and striking lightning bolts at the mortals just to watch his victims struggle and suffer. And he thought nothing about lying about afterwards. Though Brandon tried to instill in him some sense of ethical behavior, nothing seemed to take. Brandon saw no improvement. He tried to touch him daily to monitor his behavior, but increasingly the fractured readings only served to make him more concerned. Because he knew where this path led and if Bennie's future couldn't change, he would have to prevent it before it proved catastrophic for a great many people.

Of course there was always another solution. The

last resort. If he could pull it off.

Brandon sat in the waiting room bouncing one knee and shifting in the hard plastic seat. He was pretty sure they used the same seats in Guantanamo. He had tried distracting himself by playing Candy Crush on his cellphone, but even the addictive qualities of that cursed game was no help. He had been unable to sit still since he had made his decision. His stomach was cold and twisted. He stood up twice when a scrub-wearing nurse entered the room and sat back abruptly when he realized neither was Lindsay.

Finally a nurse he knew as Kim took pity on him and asked if she could help him. She left and returned a few minutes later with a message that Lindsay would be another fifteen minutes. That gave him something to do. He could check his watch obsessively.

Finally she did emerge, adjusting her purse strap on her shoulder. The weight of it pulled her shoulder down and she had to tilt the other direction to counterbalance it. Brandon stood and she saw him. She shared a tired smile as she approached. He was sure his smile in return was sickly and green. "Hi, Mark. What's the matter?"

"The matter? Oh. Nothing's wrong. No. I just thought maybe you might be hungry after your shift. I left Bennie and Liv with a bucket of The Colonel's best. I thought we could get a bite to eat and talk a bit."

She smiled again. "You seem nervous. Are you asking me out on a date?"

"A date?"

"What will Ginger say?"

Brandon opened his mouth and nothing came out. The silence grew.

"Fried chicken is not my favorite," she said

"How do you feel about burgers?"

"Love 'em."

He drove her in his cruiser over to Burger Heaven, home of the Pearly Gates Burger and they found a booth at the back of the restaurant. A waitress with hair dyed Crayola red came over to take their order.

Lindsay looked up from the menu. "I've never eaten here before. Why do they call it the Pearly Gates Burger?"

The waitress grinned. "'Cause after you've had one you'll think you've died and gone to heaven."

"With that much bacon and cheese on it that might be the case."

"True, but you'll die happy."

"I'll take one. I could use some happy."

"Better get me one, too," Brandon said.

Brandon was still feeling ill, but eating gave him something to do other than deliver the speech he had planned. He powered through the burger. Halfway through their meal Lindsay prompted him. "You wanted to talk?"

Brandon gulped down a huge bite. "Yeah. I guess I did." He lay his sandwich on the plate. "I don't know if you realize it, but I've been under a lot of stress lately."

She nodded. Her face registered concern. "I see it. I can tell," she said.

"That's why I stepped down as Chief of Police." He played with his straw, poking it up and down in his Coke. "Work is just so much... paperwork... and responsibility, and just... everything. I'm trying to keep it together, but it's invading my life. I need to make some changes."

Lindsay's face fell. "I'm so sorry. I totally understand," she said. "I've really relied heavily on your good nature. Asking you to come over every day and check on my boy and my mother. I didn't mean to assume so much. Bennie's older now, and he's really growing up. I think he's been a much better person ever since you started taking an interest in him. But of course you can stop coming by. Bennie can call 911 if there's an emergency. They'll be OK."

"Actually, that wasn't the change I was thinking of."

"Oh. I thought you were turning in your strong male role model badge."

"Nah. I still want to be there for Bennie. It's just that all the stress I'm under at work has really pulled Ginger and me apart. We never spend any time together any more. All we do is argue." Brandon's jaw tensed. He looked directly in her eyes and prayed that she would not detect the lie. "I think we really need to spend some time apart. Maybe start seeing other people."

"Oh."

"I know way back two years ago, when I started coming around, I said I wasn't planning on putting the moves on you. I really didn't intend for this to happen." *I'm going to go to hell for this,* he thought. "I have been spending a lot of time at your house, and I really have come to admire you and your family."

"Mark, I really appreciate everything you've done, but…"

Feeling sick, he blurted out the next thing, forcing it out before he could retract it. "I think maybe, I might… I love you." *Yep. Straight to hell.* He hurried on. "But if you don't feel the same way, I understand. This is all very sudden." He hung his head, feigning disappointment.

"Wow. This is kind of out of left field." She paused and started again carefully. "You know I am very fond of you, Mark. It's me. I just don't know if I'm ready." She put her hand on his arm and he used the touch to his advantage. He instantly knew what he needed to say. He felt what her response would be.

"One day you will be ready." Brandon lifted his head. "And until then, what if…"

"What?"

"I'm going to be moving out of the house. Ginger doesn't want me there anymore." *Another dead lie.* "You have an extra room. Would you consider renting it to me? It would be strictly platonic, I promise." He crossed his heart and raised his hand to emphasize. "Then I'll be there all the time to help with Bennie in the evenings and to make sure Liv gets her medication regularly. And if something develops between us, OK. If not… I won't overstep. I can be trusted. I'm a cop after all."

She was silent for minute as she looked at him, assessing the idea. The moment dragged on until it was his turn to prompt her. "It's your choice," he said.

Finally, "When are you planning on moving out?" she asked.

"Soon," he said. His hands shook. "Do you want a beer?" he asked Lindsay. He waved the waitress over.

Brandon was sitting at the kitchen table when Ginger came home from her shift at the bar. She smelled of smoke and stale beer. It clung to her clothes and in her long chestnut hair. She pulled the dirty containers from her lunch bag and took her leftover chicken bones to the trash can. He heard a sharp intake of breath as she lifted the lid. He knew what she saw there. There had been no point in hiding them. Three cans of Michelob, crushed and dead on top of the day-old garbage. He sat hunched over himself, head hanging, miserable. A fourth beer can was in front of him on the table.

He had been seven years without a drink. Seven years since he had put the bottle aside and walked away. Her disappointment radiated from her despite her silence, enveloping the room with a suffocating miasma.

"I'm sorry," he said.

After an eternity she began, "Mark—"

He cut her off before she could reach a misunderstanding. "I'm moving out." He wouldn't look at her. How could he?

The temperature in the room dropped several degrees. "What? Is there another woman? Are you seeing someone else? Who is she, Mark?"

"It's not like that."

"What is it like, then? Why are you doing this?" She gestured to include the beer in her demand for an explanation.

"I can't do this anymore. I'm not here for you. I just can't—" his voice broke, then the words he had practiced came rushing out. "You don't deserve to be with me. I'm a failure. Everything I do falls apart. I don't make enough money. We have bills piling up. I never get to see you anymore. I work days and you work nights. I can't take any time off. Duke is on my case at work. This." He lifted the Michelob and drank from it as if to prove his point. "I can't even stay sober."

Ginger was leaning against the sink her arms crossed. "Stop it. You are not a failure."

"You don't deserve a drunk who can't even support you."

"You're not a drunk. You put the bottle away before and you can do it again."

"No. You keep saying it, and it's true. I can't keep this up. You see what it's doing to me. So I have to give something up."

"So you're breaking up with *me*? Is that what you're saying? Is that what this is about?" Her hands flew up in frustration. "I meant the kid! Drop *the kid*, Mark. Not me."

He shook his head but she continued, not giving him a chance to say anything else. "No. This is not acceptable. You are obsessed. You need to see someone. A shrink. Take some pills. Whatever it takes. This kid is driving you over the edge."

She stood and began to pace the room gesticulating rapidly. "This is not acceptable," she said again. "I should have put my foot down before. I should never have let it go this far. You are sick, you know that? Sick. You quit your job for this kid! You gave up your life for this kid! Now this? No. This isn't happening."

"I have to," he countered. "Bennie is already doing nasty little things. He tortures small creatures, bugs and things, and laughs. He takes control just to see if he can and then he... he... He's just evil, I guess. I don't know. But he's working up to doing something truly horrible. I do know that. I know it every time I touch him. So I have to be there."

She pointed her finger at him, punctuating each

word. "You can't fix him."

"It's not about fixing him."

"Then what is it about, Mark? What? All this time you spend over there. With *her*. Is that what this is about? Lindsay?"

"What—? No. She's not important. No. It's about... everything." He waved his hand vaguely. "I don't know how to explain it to you. You'll never understand. Not really."

"No, you owe me an explanation. What is more important than us?"

Mark stood and reached for her. He could not use his touch to manipulate her. He would not. He could only will her to understand the way he did. "It's about saving everyone else. From him. I just—. After that Bonaventure case— when I touched him and... then Bennie—." He shuddered. "I have to leave you to keep you safe. You and everyone else. Because I love you, Ginger." He meant it when he said it to her. He did love Ginger, in a way he would never love Lindsay Callahan. But Ginger would never understand why he had to do this, nor what it cost him.

"If you love me—if you want to save me—stay with me."

"I can't. I just... can't. I have to do this. It's my final answer."

She slapped him. "This is not a game show, Mark. There is no final answer. I won't have it."

"It's not your decision to make."

Tears welled in her eyes and flowed freely down her face. "Dammit, Mark. You are a person. You deserve to have a life. A life more than waiting for some nine year old kid to go nuts. Don't you see this?"

"I have a life, Ginger. I have a purpose. There has to be a reason I have this gift. This must be it. I have to stop him, whatever it takes."

She pulled away from him. "This not a gift," she spat. "It's a curse. If you really believe he's such a monster, have him committed. Put him in a mental hospital where they can give him 24-hour care. Because you can't watch him all the time."

"But no hospital would take him. He hasn't done anything yet. And it's not illegal to be a sociopath. Not if you don't act on it.

"I'm begging you, Ginger. I'm asking you to do something impossible, I know. I'm asking you to try and understand. I can't just stand by and wait until he kills someone so I can put him away. If I don't— if I leave Bennie alone and the worst happens..."

"If you leave, the worst will have happened."

"I know," he said wretchedly. "But I have to do this."

"Don't expect me to wait forever." She crossed her arms.

"I do love you," he said. He kissed her deeply.

"Damn you, Mark Brandon," she whispered. "And damn that kid to hell." She crossed her arms and turned away.

Brandon picked up his travel bag and left the room.

The next day Brandon drove Bennie home from school and followed him into the house. His new home. In the kitchen he took off his Smith and Wesson, wrapped the belt around the hostler. He stood on his toes to reach over the fridge and put the gun in the cabinet, letting the door close softly.

He watched Bennie take his book bag to his room before pulling a beer from the fridge. He drank a deep hole in it and returned to the living room to find something mindless to fill a lonely afternoon until Lindsay came home. He felt like the world's biggest jerk manipulating her this way. It had been tough to ask her about moving in, and even worse to tell Ginger, but having the freedom to hang out on the sofa every night would make keeping tabs on Bennie so much easier. He hoped it was worth it.

He heard the screen door slam when Bennie headed outside to play and rose to pull a second beer from the fridge. He could feel the alcohol smoothing out the day's tensions, evening the surfaces before beginning his night watch.

He had neared the bottom and was contemplating the wisdom of a third beer when he heard a plaintive cry from Liv's room. "Mark?" He found the old woman crying on the edge of her bed.

"Liv? What's the matter?"

"Tom is missing. I've been looking and looking and I can't find him." She and the grey Persian were inseparable. Other than an occasional foray to the litter box or food bowl, he performed all his catly duties from a base of operations at her bedside. His disappearance made the hairs on the back of Brandon's neck rise.

"Did you check all the closets?" He didn't wait for an answer but opened the closet door himself. No Tom.

"Yes, of course. That was the first thing I did."

Brandon lifted the bed skirt to check under the bed. "Could he have slipped outside?"

"No. He would never even go near a door. He came to us after a hurricane and now he is afraid to go outside."

"Let me take a look around then, Liv." Brandon didn't promise that everything would be OK. He was pretty sure that would not be the case.

He looked out the back door but Bennie was not in sight.

Better to be thorough, Brandon thought. *The cat could be here somewhere. Maybe he got sick and holed himself up under a piece of furniture somewhere. Maybe he died of natural causes. Nobody knew how old the cat really was. Please, let that be it.*

Brandon moved from room to room, opening closet and cabinet doors. He left Bennie's room for last. It was a fairly neat room for a young boy. As always, his toys were in the toy box or placed neatly on the shelves. Books were standing up, arranged for easy browsing. The only real mess was the pile of school text books, folders and papers jumbled on the neatly made bed. He knew Lindsay didn't have time to pick up after the boy, and his grandmother wasn't mobile enough to do it. This was all Bennie. *Sign of a very ordered mind,* he thought, not for the first time. *It says a lot about the boy.* But why had he left his books scattered around? That wasn't like him.

Brandon opened the sliding door to Bennie's closet. Nothing on the floor. He moved things aside on the closet shelf. Nothing behind the stacks of Candyland, Jenga and other pristine board games. He looked at the hamper of dirty clothes. *Surely not.* With trembling hands he began to lift out the shorts and t-shirts and dirty socks, dumping them into a pile on the floor. He breathed a shaky sigh when he found the bottom, then began to return the clothes to their rightful place.

That left...

With shaking hands he opened the drawers of the dresser and lifted aside the neatly folded shirts, jeans, shorts. Layers of underwear. Pajamas, socks. And no cat. *Thank God.*

Bennie was eating Fig Newtons at the table when Brandon returned to the kitchen. He pulled a chair out and sat next to the boy. "Bennie," he began in his most authoritative tone, "Where's Tom. Tell me the truth."

The boy lifted an angelic face. *Quite the actor,* Brandon thought. He wanted to strangle the little liar.

"Isn't he in Grandma's room?"

"No, he is not. What did you do with him?"

"Nothing." The boy's eyes were still, intent and focused on Brandon. Like he was trying to will him to believe.

"Don't lie to me."

"I didn't do anything."

"Sure you did. Get up." He yanked the boy out of his chair by his arm and as he did, he reached through and *pulled.* Hard. He felt the jolt run up his arm in fizzles and starts. The boy. The cat, lifted by the back of the neck, unaware of his peril as it was zipped into the book bag. There was another wave of static in the signal. A walk in the woods. The fort Bennie had made with the neighbor kids. A culvert, a trickle of runoff and dripping water. Then the transfer to a five gallon paint bucket with a lid, holes punched in it for air. *At least he intended to keep the cat alive. For now.* A sharp pocket knife lying neatly folded next to a dirty cinder block with a broken corner on the lid of the bucket.

"Move." He propelled the boy out the kitchen door

and down the street to the empty lot where the woods began.

As they followed the path toward the fort, Brandon showed no mercy. He maintained a pace just fast enough that Bennie needed to struggle to keep up, his grip on his arm steadying the boy on the root-tied trail. There was the fort, and another path that led away towards where the creek ran under old Jack's Nursery Road. He followed it.

A muffled yowl echoed from the culvert under the road. Tom was not happy.

Brandon ducked, walking bent over to avoid hitting his head, as he pushed the boy before him into the tunnel. The growls vibrated against the metal walls as they approached the bucket.

It sat on a stone near the curved, corrugated wall. Arranged around it were low cairns of stones forming what appeared to be sacrificial altars, each adorned with the flayed skull or bones of some small animal. Brandon recognized the beak of a crow and the yellow incisors in the upper mandible of a rodent, perhaps a rat by the size, or maybe a squirrel. There were long white bones on a third pillar.

"Dammit, Bennie!" Brandon lifted the cinder block off the bucket and it began to rock as Tom fought to escape. The cat was so worked up that someone would likely get hurt trying to release him. And then they would find him seven counties over when he finally stopped running. He would have to wait until they got back in the house. Brandon picked up the bucket.

"Dammit, Bennie," he said it again. "You cannot kill things. You can't."

There was no admission on the kids' face. "I didn't."

"You were going to."

"It's just a cat."

"That's what you said about the slugs. You don't see any difference?" It was clear he did not. "Bennie, this is Tom. Your grandmother loves Tom. Why would you do this to her?"

Bennie shrugged. "I didn't do anything to *her*."

"Why, Bennie?"

"I guess I'm just bad." His posture was relaxed, as if this was nothing. It infuriated Brandon. He fought back the urge to beat the boy senseless.

"Bad is a choice, Bennie." He ground out. "Choose something else."

There was no comprehension behind the boy's eyes.

They walked back to the house in silence. Brandon didn't trust himself to speak to Bennie. Instead he used the time to try to decide how to handle this child who, it seemed, had no concept of compassion or perhaps even of attachment. If he could do this....

By the time they reached the house Brandon still had no idea what to do. He released Tom, who streaked toward refuge under Liv's dresser. "Go to your room and do your homework," he said, giving Bennie a forceful shove down the hall. "I'll discuss this with you later."

Over breakfast Lindsay heard the story from Brandon and Olivia, and she confined Bennie to his room for the next three weeks. When Brandon picked him after school, an oppressive anger followed Bennie from the passenger seat of the police cruiser to the door of the boy's room. It curled around the legs of the table at dinnertime and retreated with the boy when he returned to his room after eating. Lindsay did not refer to the incident further and Brandon still had not decided what to say to him. What could he say? "Bennie, it's not nice to torture your grandmother's cat. Vivisection is wrong." Yeah. That would work.

Commotion broke through Brandon's reverie. "Bennie, come here." There was panic in her voice as the door to Olivia's room flew open, hit the wall and bounced back shut again. A staccato burst of profanity ripped the air as the old woman pulled the door open again and emerged into the hall. Her breath came in ragged gasps and she was leaning heavily against her walker. "Bennie!" She turned toward where Brandon was rising from the recliner and as she twisted, her legs melted out from under her. She fell.

Brandon raced to her side. She was still breathing, but her lips and nail beds had a pale blue cast. She struggled to rise.

"No, Liv," Brandon said. "Just lie down. I'm going to get some help." He looked around. *Where is that kid?* "Bennie!" he bellowed.

There was a flushing sound from the end of the hall and Bennie emerged. He looked at the scene and his eyes widened.

"Bennie, go into your grandmother's room and find her pill bottles. Bring them all to me. Go!"

While he waited, he dialed 911 and gave the dispatcher all the pertinent details. When the voice on the other end of the line announced that help was on the way, Brandon yelled again. "Bennie! Hurry!"

The boy appeared at the door with a collection of bottles gathered into a pouch he had made with the hem of his t-shirt. He spilled them on the floor beside

Brandon.

There were seven bottles. Four were over-the-counter supplements. Brandon checked each of the remaining bottles. There. Nitroglycerin. But it was empty. "Did you get all the bottles, Bennie? Go look again. See if you can find another one like this." He showed him the name on the label. "Go. Hurry."

How could the nitro be empty? Lindsay had just filled the prescription.

The siren announced the arrival of the EMTs. He let them in and gave them room to work. He prayed they had arrived in time.

Lindsay joined them in the emergency bay. She hugged Bennie to herself. "Are you OK?" she asked him.

The boy nodded. "I'm fine."

"How's Mom?" she asked Brandon.

He updated her on what he knew, which wasn't much. "I wish I could have done more for her. But she was out of nitro."

"Out of nitro? How could that be? I put it on her night stand yesterday."

"I don't understand it either." He sighed. "Well, I'm going to let you have some time with her. Bennie and I will go get a Coke in the café." He stood and looked around.

He found Bennie looking between the curtains into another emergency bay. He could hear the mechanical whoosh and rattle of the ventilator. He put his hand on the boy's shoulder and felt it quiver. The boy leaning forward with intensity. "Come on, Bennie. Leave him be."

The nearly deserted cafeteria echoed with the hushed voices of a tired-looking couple as they finished picking at their food and left. A doctor walked through with a huge steaming mug of coffee and a small container of yogurt. Now, but for the woman listening to her iPod at the cash register, the place was empty.

Brandon sat watching Bennie pulling soda through his straw. He said nothing, but his eyes searched for answers to questions he didn't want to ask. Gone was the seething anger that had emanated from the boy for days. Instead, every so often Bennie would look up and smile at him tentatively, then look back down at the table. He was half-way through the enormous drink when Brandon broke the silence.

"Tell me what you did."

Bennie looked up and put on a wide-eyed face. It was a look that would melt any casual observer, but Brandon knew better than to fall it. He looked him directly in the eyes, not letting him off the hook.

"I don't know," Bennie finally said. "I didn't do it."

"What happened to your grandmother's heart pills?"

A shrug.

"You took them."

Again the boy looked away. It was his tell.

"Your mother filled that prescription just the other day. Now the pills are gone. You flushed them." No answer. "You flushed them and that is why she was chasing you and calling your name. Why did you do that?"

Another shrug.

"Do you think you're going to get in trouble?"

He did an amazing job of faking an apologetic expression.

"Tell me."

"She needed to be punished."

"Punished," Brandon repeated. "Why?"

"For tattling. When I tattle, I get punished."

"About the cat?"

"It's just a cat. I wanted to see."

"See what?"

"How it worked. It's interesting what's inside things. The muscles and the organs and things. Cats are like people, I think, but I wanted to find out for sure."

Brandon let the horror of that sink in. The little monster was studying comparative anatomy. And if he was comparing cats to people, that meant...

He put on a casual face. "How do you know how people work? Have you ever... looked inside a person?"

"No. Not yet. I've only seen shows on TV and looked at the pictures in the encyclopedia at school." He took a big swallow from his soda. "It's neat how squirrels look a lot like rats under their skin. And the bones of birds even look pretty much like squirrels and rats if you look at them right. So I think everything must look kinda the same. Squirrels, rats, birds. Even cats and people."

Brandon's stomach twisted. "Were you going to try to look at your grandmother... that way?" His voice was gray.

Bennie seemed surprised that Brandon would jump to this conclusion. "Of course not. You can't look inside while they're still alive." Brandon thought he could detect a ghostly ring of contempt in his voice. "She's alive, isn't she?"

"Good," Brandon said. "But Bennie, it's not your

job to punish anyone. You leave that to me and to your mother. And I don't want you doing any more experiments on cats in the woods, either. It's dangerous and it's wrong. OK? Promise?"

"Promise." Another gulp of soda. "You won't tell Mom?"

It would just hurt her and she wouldn't believe it anyway. She never had in the past. "If you keep your promise." He stood and held out his hand. "Come on. Let's go see your grandmother."

Brandon tried, but there was a only disjointed fizzle flowing up his arm as Bennie put his hand into Brandon's. The boy looked up questioning, "How about a dog? Can you help me find out what makes a dog alive?"

It was all Brandon could do not to crush the small bones.

Brandon was still drinking when he heard the horrific engine knock that presaged the arrival of Ginger's ancient Dodge. Lindsay was still at the hospital sitting with her mother, so Brandon had called Ginger. He needed someone to talk to, a sounding board. He had never realized how much he had come to rely on Ginger to debrief him after his battles in this whole hopeless crusade. He had treated her badly, yet she came to his aid yet again. He didn't deserve her.

He levered the recliner to the upright position and placed his beer on the kitchen table. He reached the porch in time to wave to Ginger as she waited for Timmy Greenfield, with dripping cherry snocone in hand, to pedal his trike past before she turned into the drive. As the car wound down to a clockwork tapping, she emerged.

It seemed she had grown even more heartbreakingly beautiful in the few weeks since he had moved in with Lindsay.

She leaned against the car door, her arms crossed. "You called?" she said.

He went to her, pressed her tightly against his chest and breathed in the scent of her hair. She was stiff and did not put her arms around him in return. "I wasn't sure you would come."

"I probably shouldn't have. I hate you right now," she said. "But I guess I couldn't stay away."

"I'm glad you didn't. I need you."

"*Now* you come to this realization?"

"I've always known."

"So… what? We can still date?"

He didn't laugh. He took her hand. "Come inside. I'll make you a cup of coffee."

"Lindsay home?"

"Not for an hour or two. She's still at the hospital."

Her shoulders relaxed. She broke the silence with, "I have to admit, I'm curious about this brat."

"Well, I don't think you're going to meet him today." Brandon held the door open for her.

"No, don't call him in from playing just for me. I was kidding anyway. Mostly."

"Oh, he's not playing. He's grounded," Brandon said as he ushered her into the kitchen. "You would not belie—"

Bennie's school books had been dumped in a haphazard heap in the middle of the table. They had knocked Brandon's beer over and it dripped steadily into a pool on the floor. One of the kitchen chairs had been pulled in front of the refrigerator. The kitchen seemed to tilt as his heart began to race. He reached into the cabinet above the fridge, feeling to the farthest corners. "Shit!" He swung at the chair, hurling it across the room to smash against the far wall.

"What?"

"He has my gun. Shit! *He has my gun!*"

He darted out of the kitchen, racing from room to room—it took only seconds—and returned to the kitchen. "Well, the cat is still here, but Bennie's gone. Do you still have that .38 in your glove box?"

"Yes. What's going on?"

The door slammed behind them as they raced to the car. The color drained from Ginger's face as Brandon updated her in the moments it took to check the ammunition and safety. Then he was sprinting down the street towards the vacant lot, Ginger struggling to match his ground-eating strides.

Four of the Greenfield kids turned to watch two crazy adults race past Timmy's abandoned tricycle.

At the edge of the woods a half-eaten cherry snocone melted into the dirt. He understood its significance. He heard a small gasp of distress from Ginger as she stopped, transfixed by the bright red syrup spreading over the ground. Fear pressed in upon Brandon, narrowed his world. He couldn't stop to help her process this. He knew nothing more than pumping legs and the track through the woods. As the uneven ground slowed his pace, he could hear Ginger sobbing with ragged breaths as she caught up to him.

The path seemed to lead on forever. His running made no progress. His irrational mind saw everything in slow motion, like some hokey action sequence on bad network television. He hoped that, like every TV hero, he would be in time to save the day.

The short run took forever but finally they approached the culvert. Brandon could see Bennie reaching inside his backpack, heavy with some object. A young boy, maybe four years old, backed away from him towards the gaping mouth of the pipe. Timmy Greenfield. He was sniffling, and shaking his head from side to side. "I don't want to go inside, Bennie. It's *dark.*"

"I said 'Get in,'" Bennie said, drawing out the gun. It was massive in his hand, and it wobbled as he tried to balance its weight. Timmy's eyes widened and he began to cry in earnest. "No, Bennie, No!"

Brandon stopped, holding Ginger's revolver pointed at the ground in the two-handed grip he had learned in the academy and had trained with throughout his career. It felt unnatural now. He had never needed to use it before. Not against a person. His gift had ensured he had never needed to. Now, the very first time he drew his weapon in the line of duty was against an eight year old kid. His breathing was rapid and his hands shook slightly. He deeply regretted those beers. He didn't know what to do. Years of training and he just froze. He couldn't do it.

"No, no, no, no, no!" Ginger's panicked voice came from behind him.

The boy startled and turned, lifting the gun away from his victim. *Good. He wouldn't really do it, would he?* Brandon wondered.

Ginger moved counterclockwise around the clearing, closer to where the boy cowered under Bennie's looming shadow. Her hand lifted in supplication.

"Don't do this, Bennie," she pleaded. "You don't need to do this."

Suddenly Timmy broke and ran to Ginger, grasping her around the legs in a desperate embrace. She turned to place herself between the gun and the boy.

Bennie looked at her, his eyes narrowed. "Give him back."

The boy lifted the gun. The enormity of it dwarfed his small frame.

Brandon broke free from his torpor. He began to move towards the tableaux. His police training told him—screamed at him—to shoot. *Put the boy down.* But he'd always relied on his gift to help defuse situations like this. It had always worked before. Always. "Bennie, you don't want to do this. I would have known if you meant to do this. You can stop."

"Make her give him back. His mom will never even miss him. She has six other kids." He unlocked the safety. *How did he know how to do that?* "Give him back. He's mine."

The gun wavered and settled in line with Ginger's face. *Oh, God.* He had no idea how this would end. He wished he had taken a reading from Ginger. He wished he knew if it would be OK. But no. He would never violate her privacy. Not Ginger. *Damn it.*

He tried again. "You can't. You want to be a good person, right? You can't do this and be a good person." Brandon took another step forward.

"I don't think I'm a good person. That's what you keep saying right? Choose this and you're good. Choose that and you're bad."

"Of course you can be good, Bennie. We can help you. Everyone starts out good. It's the choices you make." He wasn't sure he believed this himself anymore. He took another step. "You have to make the right choice."

"Then I guess I'm bad."

Brandon's voice rang across the clearing. The voice of The Law. "Put the gun down, Bennie."

The boy's face was still. Only his brow, pulled down in a bit of a scowl, betrayed any emotion.

"Bennie. Do what I say. Drop it. Now."

Bennie pulled the hammer back.

Brandon felt the kick against his palm. He smelled the gunpowder, saw Bennie fall. He didn't remember raising his gun.

He stared at a pool of red spread across the boy's narrow chest and onto the creek bed. The service revolver lay about a foot away from his hand, which was curled innocently like he was simply asleep.

"Oh, God." Ginger hugged the younger boy turning his head away from the scene. "Oh, Mark."

Brandon's face shattered and he folded in upon himself, his chest heaving with each ragged breath. When he could speak again, his voice was soft, almost a whisper. "You were right, Ginger."

She looked at him, uncomprehending.

"You said I couldn't stop him. And I couldn't. This is not a gift from God. It's a curse. Just like you said."

"No, Brandon. You did. You did stop him. You saved our lives."

"I never saw this. I should have known. Why didn't I know?"

"Maybe he didn't know himself, until he made the decision."

"I didn't want to do it." He paused for a long time.

His breath caught again, then he screamed his frustration and grief.

Ginger moved nearer to him, as one would approach a frightened animal. She lifted her hand to offer comfort but stopped before the contact.

"You had to. You had no choice."

Brandon rose, staring at the body of the dead boy. "No. I didn't have to take on this responsibility. I was offered a choice, and he was, too, time after time. And this is where our choices led."

He stood in silence for a moment, his head bent down. Then he inhaled, and squared his shoulders. He made another choice. Pulling his badge from his hip pocket, he threw it into the dust beside the pool of blood. He lifted Timmy to his shoulder and took Ginger's hand. "I'm done," he said. "Let's go home."

He led them back down the dark path, out of the woods and into the sunlight.

About the Author

SuperLibrarian by day and author by night, Robin Deffendall spends her work days looking up facts and her evenings weaving them into new realities. She is a member of three writers' groups, including the Wonder Chicks, and founded a well-received Writers Workshop at the Cumberland County Public Library & Information Center.

Robin has lived a relatively nomadic life until recently, and now lives in North Carolina with her three dogs and an unconscionable number of cats, all adopted during her twelve years working for a no-kill a shelter.

In her free time, Robin designs Fabrege-style eggs and is learning pysanky, the Ukrainian art of egg dying.

The stories in this anthology are side ventures to Robin's main works-in-progress. Rex Appeal tentatively expected in 2014, tells the story of a young man who can shapeshift into a Border Collie. During the course of Rex's adventures he must save the farm, save the girl, and save the day... without getting neutered in Animal Control. Her other novel, Charmer, will eventually be a traditional epic fantasy.

Made in the USA
Columbia, SC
06 December 2023

27173495R00033